Believe Me

by Kana Riley

illustrated by
Robert Byrd

Scott Foresman

Editorial Offices: Glenview, Illinois • New York, New York
Sales Offices: Reading, Massachusetts • Duluth, Georgia
Glenview, Illinois • Carrollton, Texas • Menlo Park, California

Howdy!

Augustus P. Frogbelly here.

Sit right down and I'll tell you a story. You may not believe it. Some don't. It's up to you.

Sign Up
Golf Lessons
Here

Now, before I start, take a look over there. See the prize trophy? I'll tell you how I won that thing.

It was the last hole of the Pebble
Pond Golf Tournament. I used to
compete in a lot of contests back then.

Well, I was pretty far off the lead.
To win, I needed a hole in one.

Not many people can get the ball in
the hole with one swing. But I figured
I'd give it a try.

I stepped up to the tee. I swung.
And that ball started to sail. Up. Up.
Right toward the green. It was
looking beautiful.

Then . . . a problem! A big problem!
Out of the blue, a twister showed
up. It dipped down and scooped my
ball right out of the air.

That twister was going a mile a
minute. No joke! It took my ball
halfway across town. Then it dropped it.
The ball landed on a circus tent. It
bounced as if it had springs.

Well, I was in luck. Just then a duck flew by. And whoop! It caught the ball. Honest! August P. Frogbelly does not tell jokes.

That old duck was flying pretty fast. But she didn't look where she was going.

Mallard Airlines
Why waddle when
you can fly?

Blam! Next thing you know, that
fool bird had rammed smack into a
hot air balloon. Big problem!

The duck dropped the ball. The ball
fell like a rock into the basket. That
would have been okay except the
balloon had sprung a leak.

It was going down! Another big
problem!

I hollered to the guy in the balloon. "Throw down a rope!"

He didn't have much choice. So he tossed me a line.

I grabbed hold of it. I started to run.

Splash! The balloon landed in the middle of the pond. It smacked the water hard—so hard that it sent the ball flying . . .

right into the hole.

"Hole in one!" cried the judge. "The prize goes to Augustus P. Frogbelly."

I, you may recall, am Augustus P. Frogbelly.

So that, my friend, is how I came to have that trophy.

As I said, you may not believe me. It's up to you.